The Little Ant

by David Novak
illustrated by David Drotleff

How The Little Ant came to be

The more stories I tell, the more delightful it is to see how a story can grow and change from one telling to the next. If you've ever played a game of "telephone" you know how easily a simple phrase changes as it is passed from one person to the next.

In the same way, stories change as they are passed on. I have found many versions of *The Little Ant* over the years. The oldest version I have found in print is *In The Reign of Coyote*, written in 1905.

My version of *The Little Ant* combines two of my favorite types of story: a "circle" story and a "cumulative" story. The circle story goes round in a circle, like the Japanese tale *The Stonecutter* or the song "Itsy Bitsy Spider." It ends where it began. The cumulative story picks up events or characters as the story develops, like the story of *The Old Woman and Her Pig* or *The Gingerbread Man*. Just as a snowball rolling down a hill gets larger and larger, the repeated phrase going through the story gets longer and longer with each new character.

I am interested in *The Little Ant* (and stories like it) because it speaks of something we all need to learn: that every action we take affects someone or something. If we want to find the cause of our troubles, instead of looking for someone else to blame, maybe we should look at our own actions and consider how we can effect a change for the better.

—*David Novak*

Let Me Tell You a Story!

To Corky and Jack,
who in many small ways make a big difference.

Published by Riverbank Press
801 94th Avenue North, St. Petersburg, Florida 33702

Copyright © 1994 by Riverbank Press,
a division of PAGES, Inc.

Printed in the United States of America

2 4 6 8 10 9 7 5 3

ISBN 0-87406-689-1

There once was an ant, a busy little ant, with a great big giant
appetite. One day, as he scurried home for dinner with a large
crust of bread, a snowflake suddenly landed in his path.
Whoosh!
The little ant slipped and fell.

"Snowflake!" said the little ant. "You're a big bully! You did that on purpose and I hurt my leg! Well, you won't get away with it!"

Before the snowflake could say a word, the little ant dragged him all the way to the jail.

"Sheriff," said the little ant, "arrest this snowflake! He fell in my way and made me slip and fall. I hurt my leg!"

"Is that so?" said the sheriff.

He looked at the snowflake. "You fell out of the sky to make the little ant slip and hurt his leg? You big bully! What do you have to say for yourself?"

The snowflake trembled and said, "I'm not a bully. I fell from the sky because I had to escape from the real bully, who tried to melt me into a drop of water. Don't arrest me. Arrest the sun!"

"Is that so?" said the sheriff. He looked out the window and called, "Sun! Get in here!"

Into the jail came the sun.

"Sun," said the sheriff, "you tried to melt the snowflake, who made the little ant slip and hurt his leg? You big bully! What do you have to say for yourself?"

The sun flickered and said, "I'm not a bully. I had to shine bright and hot because the real bully tried to cover me up. Don't arrest me. Arrest the cloud!"

"Is that so?" said the sheriff. He looked out the window and called, "Cloud! Get in here!"

Into the jail came the cloud.

"Cloud," said the sheriff, "you covered the sun, who tried to melt the snowflake, who made the little ant slip and hurt his leg? You big bully! What do you have to say for yourself?"

The cloud sighed and said, "I'm not a bully. I covered the sun because the real bully pushed me into it. Don't arrest me. Arrest the wind!"

"Is that so?" said the sheriff. He looked out the window and called, "Wind! Get in here!"

Into the jail came the wind.

"Wind," said the sheriff, "you pushed the cloud, who covered the sun, who tried to melt the snowflake, who made the little ant slip and hurt his leg? You big bully! What do you have to say for yourself?"

The wind whined and said, "I'm not a bully. I blew into the cloud because the real bully stopped me. He was too tough to pass through, and so I had to go around him. Then I bumped into the cloud. Don't arrest me. Arrest the wall!"

"Is that so?" said the sheriff. He looked out the window and called, "Wall! Get in here!"

Into the jail came the wall.

"Wall," said the sheriff, "you stopped the wind, who pushed the cloud, who covered the sun, who tried to melt the snowflake, who made the little ant slip and hurt his leg? You big bully! What do you have to say for yourself?"

The wall groaned, "I'm not a bully. I have to be as thick and tough as I can be because the real bully nibbles at me. He nibbled a hole in me! Don't arrest me. Arrest the mouse!"

"Is that so?" said the sheriff. He looked out the window and called, "Mouse! Get in here!"

Into the jail came the mouse.

"Mouse," said the sheriff, "you nibbled a hole in the wall, who stopped the wind, who pushed the cloud, who covered the sun, who tried to melt the snowflake, who made the little ant slip and hurt his leg? You big bully! What do you have to say for yourself?"

The mouse squeaked, "Eeek! I'm not a bully. I had to nibble a hole in the wall so I could hide because the real bully chased me. Don't arrest me. Arrest the cat!"

"Is that so?" said the sheriff. He looked out the window and called, "Cat! Get in here!"

Into the jail came the cat.

"Cat," said the sheriff, "you chased the mouse, who nibbled a hole in the wall, who stopped the wind, who pushed the cloud, who covered the sun, who tried to melt the snowflake, who made the little ant slip and hurt his leg? You big bully! What do you have to say for yourself?"

The cat purred and said, "Mmmmm. I'm not a bully. I chased the mouse because the real bully made me. He scared me into chasing him. Don't arrest me! Arrest the man!"

"Is that so?" said the sheriff. He looked out the window and called, "Man! Get in here!"

Into the jail came the man.

"Man," said the sheriff, "you scared the cat, who chased the mouse, who nibbled a hole in the wall, who stopped the wind, who pushed the cloud, who covered the sun, who tried to melt the snowflake, who made the little ant slip and hurt his leg? You big bully! What do you have to say for yourself?"

The man frowned and said, "I'm not a bully. I scared the cat into chasing the mouse because I thought the mouse was stealing from me. But now I can see that the real bully is standing right here."

The man pointed a finger at the ant. "Look! He's holding a crust of my bread! So don't arrest me. Arrest the little ant!"

"So *you're* the one who started this whole thing!" the sheriff said to the little ant. "You stole from the man, who scared the cat, who chased the mouse, who nibbled a hole in the wall, who stopped the wind, who pushed the cloud, who covered the sun, who tried to melt the snowflake, who made you slip and hurt your leg! What do you have to say for yourself?"

The little ant looked around the crowded jail and said, "Well . . . umm . . . I'm sorry. I guess I wasn't thinking."

The sheriff crossed his arms and looked at the little ant. "I'm glad you're sorry," the sheriff said. Then he looked at everyone and said,